Baby Penguin

Animal Adventures

sequoia children's publishing

Ark! Ark! At the frozen seaside, the penguins greet each other with loud barking noises. Father Penguin returns from a swim in the sea. He builds up speed until he can leap out onto the ice. Then he shakes the cold water off his feathers. It is now his turn to stay close to the nest so Mother Penguin can go fishing.

Mother Penguin climbs from the nest. Her movements wake her baby. Baby Penguin blinks her bright black eyes.

Baby Penguin's a bit of a slowpoke. When she was born, she took half a day to break out of her shell. It takes a long time for her to eat a meal. And even though she is three weeks old, she has never left her nest.

Baby Penguin looks around. Penguins are everywhere, and they are all squawking loudly! They sure are noisy.

Penguins are birds, but they cannot fly. Baby Penguin's wings are really more like flippers. Baby Penguin will be able to fly through the water with her special wings.

Each family of penguins guards its nest. If a stranger gets too close, Father Penguin stretches his neck. His neck feathers fluff out. He points his head up to the sky and grunts. Baby Penguin stretches her neck and grunts, too.

Father Penguin and his baby tell the stranger to keep away from their home.

Father Penguin protected Baby Penguin when she was just an egg, too. He held the egg on top of his feet so it wouldn't touch the ice for almost two months. A flap of warm belly skin covered the egg and kept it warm.

Baby Penguin's parents must go fishing often to catch enough food for their tiny baby. They will have to leave her for a while. Baby Penguin's mother and father bring her to a group of young penguins. She follows along, waddling slowly.

Baby Penguin will be safe in this group. Some older penguins will watch for danger. They circle around the babies and shelter them from the icy cold winds.

If an enemy approaches, the adult penguins will beat their wings and screech to scare the enemy.

Baby Penguin snuggles with the others. She begins to fall asleep. Baby Penguin does not notice the group is moving away from her. She wakes up and sees a bird diving at her!

Luckily for Baby Penguin, an older penguin is nearby. The big penguin runs toward Baby Penguin, waving his flippers and barking loudly. He scares the bird away!

Baby Penguin hasn't learned how to escape danger yet. Soon Mother and Father Penguin will teach her how to swim really fast through the water and away from danger.

Baby Penguin goes back to the group. She is frightened and very hungry. Suddenly, she hears her father calling to her! Will he find her? Baby Penguin is lost in a crowd of fuzzy little penguins that look just like her.

Baby Penguin lifts her head and barks as loudly as she can. Her parents hear her over all the other noise. They find her!

Baby Penguin is happy to return to the nest with Mother and Father Penguin. She knows it is time for them to feed her the fish that they have caught in the sea.

A few weeks have passed. Baby Penguin has new feathers. Now she looks like an adult. Baby Penguin flaps her flippers. She seems like she is ready to go somewhere. So do the other penguins. They've formed a big group near the water's edge.

Baby Penguin follows them. She uses her small flippers to slide across the ice on her belly.

Baby Penguin quickly discovers that sliding is the best way to get around on the cold snow and ice. Penguins do this by using their round bellies as toboggans.

It is time for the young penguins' first swim in the sea. Baby Penguin is one of the last to dive in. She's really swimming fast! Baby Penguin is no longer such a slowpoke!